SNOWBOARD
BALANCING ACT

BY JAKE MADDOX

text by
Monica Roe

STONE ARCH BOOKS
a capstone imprint

Published by Stone Arch Books, an imprint of Capstone.
1710 Roe Crest Drive, North Mankato, Minnesota 56003
capstonepub.com

Library of Congress Cataloging-in-Publication Data is available on the Library of Congress website.
ISBN: 9781666344790 (hardcover)
ISBN: 9781666344837 (paperback)
ISBN: 9781666344844 (ebook PDF)

Summary: For twelve-year-old Bristol, being on the slopes means ultimate freedom. As an adaptive snowboarder and a junior instructor, the upcoming PowderX Games are a chance to show her parents how serious she is about the sport. But juggling boarding and teaching with homework and vision therapy for her physiologic diplopia is harder than Bristol thought. When her parents announce that she'll have to drop some of her snowboarding commitments if she doesn't do well on an important exam, Bristol is determined to prove that she can do it all.

Editorial Credits
Editor: Alison Deering; Designer: Tracy Davies; Media Researcher: Svetlana Zhurkin; Production Specialist: Katy LaVigne

Consultant Credits
Special thanks to Chris Bode and Dr. Kamey Kapp

Image Credits
Shutterstock: Brocreative, 2–3, 92–93, 94–95, Isniper, 88–89, 90–91, Sergey Mironov, cover, Sergey Novikov, back cover and throughout, Volodymyr Goinyk, 1 and throughout

All internet sites appearing in back matter were available and accurate when this book was sent to press.

TABLE OF CONTENTS

CHAPTER I

PURE POWDER

"Bristol! Help!"

With a shower of powder, Bristol Budnikas halted in front of the other boarder. "You okay, Jamila?"

The little girl rolled over. "I wiped out!" Jamila declared proudly. She sat up and spit out a mouthful of snow.

Bristol grinned. When Jamila had first started lessons, she'd been scared of the slopes. She'd worried about trying even the bunny hill without holding on to someone. Now her confidence—and daring— seemed to grow every week.

"You're doing great," Bristol said proudly. "Just remember to keep your weight a little more centered, okay? Now, come on. Last one back buys hot chocolate!"

Jamila returned the grin and grabbed Bristol's outstretched glove. "How about the coach buys hot chocolate?" she joked.

Bristol felt a flash of pride at the word *coach*. She had been snowboarding her whole life. She'd practically grown up on the mountain. But when she was nine, she'd been in a car accident that caused a head injury. She'd mostly recovered—except for some lasting vergence dysfunction.

Ever since, Bristol had battled vision issues— including on the mountain. Her eyes could stay steady and focused for a short amount of time, especially looking at things up close. But eventually they tried to go in opposite directions.

It could be a real hassle—eye fatigue, headaches, double vision, trouble judging how far away things were. It even threw off her balance sometimes. The customized goggles Bristol wore had special lenses that helped her eyes maintain focus when she had to glance between obstacles on the slopes. They helped some, but it wasn't a perfect fix.

It had taken Bristol a long time to adjust to boarding with her new limitations. But she'd done it. Maybe she couldn't be as fast or aggressive on the slopes as she once was, but she was working on it.

And now she was helping other kids. This was her first year as a junior volunteer coach with the Tiny Titans, Roman Run's adaptive skiing and snowboarding program for kids.

Bristol handed Jamila her outrigger poles. They had tiny skis on the bottom that gave extra support for skiers or boarders who needed help balancing.

"Don't forget these!" she said.

"I bet I won't need them for long!" Jamila declared.

"Especially now that you've got your fancy new leg," Bristol agreed. "Did you decide on some stickers to decorate it?"

Jamila had gotten a new leg from her prosthetist last week. She had been so excited to show everyone how lightweight and high-tech it was. Most importantly, it was pink—Jamila's favorite color.

Together, Bristol and Jamila cruised back to the rest of the group.

"Nice wipeout, Jamila!" Greta, the head coach, said. She grinned and poked the bobble of Jamila's fuzzy hat. Then she turned to Bristol. "I was just telling the kids about that sweet tripod you did the other day. They want a demo!"

"Show us!" Aurora piped up, bouncing on her tiny blue skis.

Jyoti, the junior coach paired with Aurora, steadied the little girl. It was just Aurora's fourth time skiing. She was still getting the hang of keeping her balance on her left side, which was weaker than her right while on skis.

The other kids joined in. "Show! Show!"

Bristol gave in, laughing. "Okay, okay."

She undid one binding and towed her board to a smooth stretch of snow a little way up the slope. Then she locked back in and started down the hill.

Bristol picked up speed, sliding on her toe edge, then turned until she was facing uphill. She closed her eyes, planted both hands on the ground, and shifted her weight back onto the tail of her board.

She heard the kids gasp, then cheer, as the nose of her board popped into the air. Powder swirled around Bristol's face as she slid down the slope, her board almost upright, one edge and both hands against the ground in a perfect triangle.

Perfect balance, Bristol thought triumphantly. She used her core muscles and pushed hard to pop onto her feet.

"That was sooooo cool!" Jamila cried when Bristol rejoined them.

Bristol grinned. The tripod had been fun—but tough— to master. Flipping upside down quickly often made her dizzy. But she was determined not to let her sometimes-misbehaving eyes get in her way. She'd practiced and practiced until she could do the trick with her eyes closed.

"It'll be even cooler when you're doing it one day," Bristol told Jamila.

Greta checked her smartwatch. "Better call it a day," she said.

Bristol, Jyoti, and Greta helped the kids the rest of the way down the hill. The kids' parents waited at the bottom.

"I'm going to do a few more runs," Jyoti said when the last of the kids had gone. "Want to come with?"

Bristol shook her head. "Love to," she said, "but I need to grab a snack before Mom picks me up."

Her stomach growled, reminding her she'd skipped lunch to finish her homework. But at least that meant she wouldn't have to do it tonight.

"Next time, for sure," she added.

"Okay!" Jyoti waved and headed toward the chairlifts.

Bristol and Greta stashed their boards in the rack outside the lodge, then went inside. A warm fire crackled in the stone fireplace, and delicious smells came from the little restaurant.

"You're doing great with the kids," Greta said as they walked.

Bristol felt a rush of pride. "Thanks. I'm loving it."

She'd been super excited to work with the adaptive program. Learning to snowboard again after her own injury had felt so empowering, especially after some doctors had warned her that she might not be able to.

But Bristol had been determined. She'd always felt so *right* snowboarding—doing anything athletic really.

Unlike the rest of her super-academic family, Bristol felt at home on the slopes. There was no way she'd give that up. Even if she'd had to adjust her goals of competing one day, coaching had given her a whole new feeling of purpose and passion.

Bristol wanted to give other kids that same feeling. It had been amazing so far—despite having to balance the extra commitment with school and her own snowboarding.

"Check it out." Greta pointed to a paper on the wall as they entered the food line.

Bristol looked at the flyer. It was for the PowderX Games, an adaptive competition held at a different mountain each year.

"Wow, they're finally having it at Roman's Run this year," she said. The thought of the competition happening at her home mountain was exciting. "But it's not like I could ever really compete," she pointed out.

Adaptive snowboarding was a growing sport, but it still didn't include all athletes. The International Paralympic Committee only had classifications for snowboarders with arm and leg impairments or amputations. The World Snowboarding Federation had more categories, but none that exactly matched Bristol's specific limitations.

Greta frowned. "I know. But it's important for the officials to see more adaptive athletes. We're trying to put together a bunch of exhibition runs this year. Boarders do a run but don't get a competition score. We'll definitely do one with the Tiny Titans. Would you be up for extra classes to help get them ready?"

Bristol grinned. "Definitely," she said. Then she read the date on the flyer. "Wow, only a month away."

Pretty close to exams, she thought privately.

Bristol was in eighth grade, but her parents had her taking several advanced classes to prepare for high school. Keeping up with all the reading and quizzes was a lot more work than she'd expected, especially with coaching added to her responsibilities.

But helping get the kids—and herself!—ready for an exhibition run sounded way more fun.

"I'm sure I can find the time," Bristol said. "You entering one of the main events?"

"You bet!" Greta said as they collected their food.

Bristol wasn't surprised. At twenty-three, Greta was one of the best skiers around. She made whizzing through a mogul field look like flying.

As they sat by the fireplace, Bristol's phone chimed. It was her mom.

In the parking lot. Can't be late for your appointment.

Bristol groaned. *I forgot about vision therapy!*

She had an appointment at least once a week. But after a long day at school and on the slopes, she *really* didn't feel like riding forty-five minutes to her appointment. The clinic's evening hours were convenient but made for a long day.

Bristol stowed her phone. "My mom's outside. I'll have to take my food to go."

"Think about doing a run yourself," Greta said.

"I will," Bristol assured her. She hurried toward the door to the parking lot, then realized her snowboard was still stashed in the rack out back.

Whoops! Bristol thought as she raced back through the lodge to retrieve it. *Hope Mom isn't too upset if we're a couple minutes late.*

CHAPTER 2

VIRTUAL SLOPES

"Think fast!" Bristol cried.

The ball whizzed through the air toward Sanjay, her vision therapist. He held up a hand and caught it. The string that attached it to the ceiling directly overhead dangled loosely.

"Maybe you should go out for softball instead of snowboarding," Sanjay joked. "Ready?"

Bristol nodded and focused on the ball. It was a special one used in vision therapy to help with visual tracking. Big and small letters were printed on it in a random pattern.

"Go for it," she said.

Sanjay pushed the ball hard, making it swing from its string like a tiny tetherball.

Bristol watched the ball intently. When they'd first started this exercise, she'd been sure the ball would whack her in the nose.

But Sanjay was a pro. He always kept it whirling in a perfect arc.

The ball circled her, whizzing past at eye level. Bristol focused hard on the letters as they flew by. Ever since her head injury, her eyes had trouble working together—especially if she was overtired or stressed.

Bristol shouted letters as fast as she could make them out. "G . . . X . . . P, B!"

"Break time," Sanjay said after a few minutes. He stopped the ball. "You feel okay?"

Bristol rubbed her eyes. They seemed more tired than usual, probably because of all the reading she'd had for school lately.

"Yeah," she said. "I came straight from the slopes today." She told Sanjay about chasing Jamila and how proud the girl was about wiping out on her own.

Sanjay laughed. "Sounds like you're really enjoying coaching," he said.

"I love it," Bristol said eagerly. "It's so cool seeing how confident the kids are when they figure out what they can do."

"How has your vision been on the slopes?" Sanjay asked. He led the way to a different part of the therapy gym. "Your goggles still working well?"

Bristol nodded. "Hopefully I'll be able to give them a real workout soon," she said. "There's an adaptive competition at Roman's Run next month. Just have to convince Mom to let me spend the extra time on the slopes to get ready."

Sanjay, who was setting up a virtual reality program on the wall screen, nodded. "She still worried about coaching taking time away from school?" he asked.

"Yes!" Bristol sighed. "No matter how many times I tell her I can handle it, she doesn't understand. Dad, either."

Being a junior coach meant everything to Bristol, but her parents didn't seem totally on board. They were both college professors and had always supported her snowboarding for fun, but they'd also made it clear that school came first.

It hadn't been easy to convince them to let her coach. Especially since her injury had caused her to miss so much school. If her grades started to suffer, Bristol knew she'd quickly lose slope time.

Sanjay nodded sympathetically. He'd heard about this at previous visits.

"That sounds tough," he said, turning on the screen and handing Bristol the VR goggles. "I know how hard it can be when you and your parents want different things."

Bristol sighed and slipped on the goggles. "It'll be fine. I just have to show them I can balance everything."

"Speaking of balance . . ." Sanjay said. "Surprise!"

Bristol grinned as a virtual mountain and starting gate appeared on the screen. "Nice!"

They spent the rest of the session on the virtual slope, working on different exercises. They were all designed to help both of Bristol's eyes track, focus, and accommodate together.

Sanjay gradually adjusted the program to give Bristol harder and harder challenges. At one point she even had to use her eye muscle movements to intercept snowballs that suddenly appeared in her field of vision. It was almost like really being on the slopes—just not as cold.

"That was great," Bristol said as they finished. "And tough!" Her eyes were super tired, which wasn't unusual after a therapy session.

As they went to the lobby to check out, Sanjay handed her paper with a log-in written on it.

"We're using a new app in the clinic," he explained. "Instead of homework on paper each week, now I can just send you exercises via the app. You can log them as you do them, and we can track progress each week."

"Great," Bristol groaned. "More homework!"

Sanjay grinned. "I know, I know. But we think it'll help patients remember to do their exercises between clinic visits. Besides, who doesn't love a chance to use their phone?"

Bristol promised to download the app, then went outside. Her mom was there waiting.

"How was your session?" Mom asked as Bristol got into the car.

"It was fine. Sanjay had a new virtual snowboarding activity. Almost as good as the real thing!" she joked.

Then she remembered she hadn't told her mom about the PowderX Games.

"By the way, there's a competition coming up at the mountain," Bristol said. "Greta asked me to help with the kids' exhibition event."

She hesitated. "I was thinking about maybe doing an exhibition event too."

Her mom frowned. "I don't know," she said. "What about that grade on your German test last week? You know a B minus is not acceptable."

"It was just one test!" Bristol protested. "And this is important. There aren't enough adaptive snowboarders as it is. We have to support each other!"

"You're in advanced classes now, Bristol," her mom said. "Grades matter."

I'm only in eighth grade, Bristol thought to herself. But that didn't seem to matter to her parents. All they cared about was school.

"We made a deal," she reminded her mom quietly. "I can snowboard and teach as long as I can balance it with school and everything else."

"Balance it *and* keep your grades up," her mom added. "It may be 'just one test,' but organization is key to making sure things don't slide."

Bristol held up the paper from Sanjay. "I am organized. See? We're even getting a new app to keep track of all my vision therapy exercises."

Mom looked unconvinced, but Bristol was determined.

I can handle it all, she thought. *I just have to prove it.*

CHAPTER 3

ON THE MOUNTAIN

Bristol fidgeted eagerly as the chairlift carried her up the mountain. It was Sunday afternoon. She and Jyoti had met Lita, a friend from school, for a slopes day.

Finally! Bristol thought as she rose over the evergreens. She'd waited all week to let loose.

One chair ahead, Jyoti turned to wave. "Bet you lunch that I beat you down the mountain!" she joked.

I don't care who beats who, Bristol thought excitedly. *As long as we're on our boards.*

After a long week of balancing school, homework, and after-school coaching sessions, an afternoon boarding with friends sounded great. With everything else going on, she hadn't really gotten onto the mountain on her own much yet this season. She'd even been up late doing homework last night so she could spend today on the slopes.

When the chairlift reached the top, Bristol stood and pushed off. She cruised down to join her friends at the top of the slopes.

Lita adjusted her silver helmet. "Where to?"

Bristol and Jyoti studied the signs posted at the fork. The slopes at Roman Run were named for ancient goddesses and gods. To the right were Ceres and Vesta—wide, gentle, green slopes for beginners. Left through the woods were Diana, Apollo, and Bacchus—all intermediate-level blue runs.

"Warm up on the greens?" Jyoti suggested. "Then head to the harder ones?"

Bristol and Lita nodded, and the girls pushed off down Vesta. It was a great warm-up run, full of easy hills and wide turns. The weekend crowd had mostly left for the day, and there was plenty of space to spread out.

Bristol's board cut wide curves in the powder as she carved down the run. She stared straight ahead, feeling confident and in control.

But then ahead of her, Jyoti's bright-red parka suddenly split into two parkas in her field of vision.

Oh, come on! Bristol thought.

She blinked a few times and concentrated. Her eyes always had trouble focusing on faraway objects if she looked at them too quickly. Especially after reading or using a computer—or staying up far too late doing both.

She'd had several surgeries after her head injury. Her eyes had gotten better over time—and regular vision therapy and her prism-lensed goggles helped—but they'd never fully recovered.

Bristol could usually manage on the slopes. As long as they weren't too crowded and her eyes weren't too fatigued. But today, as she looked away down the hill, her vision stayed doubled, even when she tried hard to correct it.

Too much computer time last night, Bristol scolded herself. Then she realized, *Ugh, forgot to do my eye exercises too.*

She'd been forgetting to do them a lot lately. There just never seemed to be enough time to get everything done.

Bristol made a mental note to activate the app Sanjay had given her. She needed to get back on track with her exercises. Her eyes were definitely not seeing the slopes as well as they should be.

But for now, there are more important things to think about! Bristol reasoned.

After all, she'd come up with plenty of tricks to help herself accommodate when she needed. The double vision came and went. If it got too bad, she could always close one eye to make it down the hill.

Bristol cruised around a curve that slanted up sideways, crouching low to keep her balance. She focused on a spot only a few feet ahead to keep her vision steady. As she crested the bowl of the little hill, she shifted her weight quickly and popped the front of her board into a perfect ollie.

Yes! Bristol cheered silently. Sticking a landing always made her feel fierce and free. Invincible.

She imagined herself doing the same on an exhibition run at the PowderX Games. Maybe the banked slalom, which was wide and curvy. She just had to convince her parents to let her participate.

After a few more runs down Vesta and Ceres, the girls rode the lift back up. This time they headed left through the woods to the tougher blue runs.

They started with Apollo, which was wide-open but full of steeper slopes that often iced up in the midday winter sun. Then they headed over to Bacchus, full of wild drops and curves.

At the bottom of the run, Bristol brushed powder off her goggles and hat. Bacchus had been tougher than Vesta. She'd definitely closed one eye a few times to see things far away without the doubling. But still, being out on the slopes felt amazing.

Bristol glanced at the time. She had half an hour before her dad picked her up.

"Want to finish up on Minerva?" she asked.

"You know it!" Jyoti replied.

The girls headed for the lift. Minerva was challenging. Getting down required crossing a broad field of moguls that made the slope look like a moon landscape.

As they worked their way through the mogul field, Bristol's eyes felt really tired. The number of moguls she saw kept shifting when she looked too far down the slope—and even closer up than usual.

No biggie, Bristol told herself. *Just need to take it a bit slower.*

"Everything okay?" Jyoti asked as they cleared the moguls.

Bristol gave her a thumbs-up. "Just a little tired," she promised.

The girls cruised along the tree line that separated the bottom of Minerva from the top of the bunny slope. Just then, someone on the bunny slope shouted.

"Bristol!"

Bristol checked for cross traffic on the slope, then crossed slowly through the trees. On the other side, she saw Jamila and her mom. Jamila was sprawled in the snow, giggling.

Bristol grinned and boarded over. "Did you wipe out again?" she asked, helping Jamila's mom pull the little girl up.

"Sure did!" Jamila declared. "Mom let me try without outriggers!"

"You mean you ditched them and bolted before I could say no!" Jamila's mom rolled her eyes but grinned as she held up the small poles.

Bristol laughed. "Of course she did."

"She's gained so much confidence since starting classes with you, Bristol," Jamila's mom added. "She's always talking about how great you are."

Bristol blushed. "I love boarding with Jamila," she said. "Even if I spend half my time chasing you, superstar." She pretended to glare at the little girl, who grinned back.

Hearing the praise from Jamila's mom made Bristol feel proud. Even though it was tough, it really was worth it to try and balance everything.

* * *

As Bristol got ready for bed that night, she was still thinking about what Jamila's mom had said. Then her phone chimed. It was a text from Lita.

How about that book Mr. Hockley assigned? Couldn't put it down!

Shoot! Bristol realized. She'd completely forgotten about the extra assigned reading for global studies class.

Bristol jumped out of bed to get the book. As she grabbed it, a paper fell from her backpack with it. It was the note from Sanjay with the setup instructions for her vision therapy app.

Ugh! Bristol thought. *No more putting it off. I'll set it up first thing tomorrow.*

She settled back into bed and opened the book. If she read one chapter tonight and woke up early tomorrow, maybe she could get the reading done.

But ten minutes after she started, the book slipped from her hands. Bristol had fallen asleep.

CHAPTER 4

SCHOOL STRUGGLES

When her alarm went off, Bristol sat up with a start. The open book tumbled off her chest and on to the floor.

"Ugh!" she groaned. She'd fallen asleep reading!

"Rise and shine!" Dad called through her door. "You ready for the day?"

Bristol jumped up. "Ready!"

She rushed through getting dressed, made a to-go smoothie and headed for the door.

"You're leaving early," Mom said as Bristol headed out twenty minutes before she usually did.

"Thought I'd get some extra studying in," Bristol said.

Not a complete fib, she thought guiltily.

Bristol crunched through the snow to the bus stop. She read while she waited, during the ride to school, and during homeroom. Luckily, Mr. Hockley led a class discussion on the reading instead of giving a quiz.

Bristol tried to pay attention, but it was hard not to look out the window when it started snowing. The air was filled with thick flakes, and Roman's Run was just visible through the window.

"Bristol?" Mr. Hockley called.

"Sorry!" Bristol said sheepishly. "What was the question?"

Mr. Hockley smiled. "I've got snow fever myself. But let's try and focus, okay?"

Bristol nodded, but silently she added, *That's my problem. Too many things to focus on.*

* * *

The week flew by. Bristol's teachers assigned lots of homework, and on Wednesday she had an English test. When she'd handed in her paper, Bristol had a sinking feeling she should have studied more.

On Thursday, she headed to Roman's Run after school. There were no students today. Instead, the junior coaches had a training session to learn about some new adaptive gear.

"This is a DuoRider," Greta explained. "Can anyone guess which sorts of disabilities it might help on the slopes?"

Bristol studied the kid-size setup. It was similar to the seated frames for skiers who were paralyzed. But this frame looked taller, a little less supportive.

Bristol thought about Aurora, from Saturday's class. "Is it for kids who maybe aren't paralyzed . . . but have some weakness?" she guessed. "Like cerebral palsy?"

"Exactly!" Greta high-fived her. "The DuoRider can help kids with CP, who are often weaker or tighter on one side. The frame gives them some support—but not more than they need."

"Would this be something we could use with Aurora?" Jyoti piped up. She'd clearly had the same thought as Bristol. "She can stand, technically, but it takes so much effort and her balance is unpredictable."

Greta nodded. "You got it! This was just donated. I can't wait for Aurora to try it. It will help her sort of half-sit, half-stand while she rides. I think, with practice, she could even use it on her own!"

Bristol listened intently during the rest of the session. Learning about the equipment, which could help almost anyone get out on the slopes, was so interesting.

"Remember," Greta told them, "an adaptation is just something that helps someone get what they need to do what they love."

After the session, Bristol helped Greta and the others stow the adaptive gear. Then she headed to the lodge. The PowderX Games flyer was still there.

I need to get an answer from Mom and Dad about participating—and helping with the kids' exhibition. Bristol reminded herself. *SOON.*

* * *

On Friday, Bristol woke up feeling excited. Last night—after a whole lot of coaxing—her parents had cautiously agreed to let her participate in the upcoming games. Now there was just one more school day—plus vision therapy after—then two days on the slopes!

But in last period, things took a turn. Bristol's English teacher, Ms. Lopez-Sørensen, handed back the tests from earlier in the week.

Bristol groaned when she saw the C+ written in red on hers. If her parents saw this grade, there was a good chance they'd change their minds about letting her participate in the games.

Maybe I won't tell them, Bristol thought.

As the dismissal bell rang, Ms. Lopez-Sørensen came to Bristol's desk. The other students hurried out.

"Everything okay, Bristol?" the teacher asked. "That's not your usual grade."

No kidding, Bristol thought.

"I'm okay. Just . . . busy with everything," she said. "I started coaching at Roman's Run this year."

Ms. Lopez-Sørensen nodded. "I know how hard you've been working with your students on the slopes," she said. "My nephew loves your class— he never stops talking about it."

Bristol had almost forgotten that Liam, one of her most energetic students, was Ms. Lopez-Sørensen's nephew.

Bristol's teacher looked sympathetic but firm. "It must be a lot to balance. Are you taking on too much?"

Just what I need, Bristol thought. *Someone else thinking I can't handle it all!*

"I'm good," she said. "Just need to study more next time."

"There's another test in two weeks," Ms. Lopez-Sørensen said. "Dazzle me then, okay?"

The week before the games, Bristol thought. *Great.*

н н н

"How's school going?" Sanjay asked at Bristol's next vision therapy appointment.

Bristol groaned. "Don't ask!"

Sanjay winced sympathetically. "Sounds like we should start with something fun today."

Soon Bristol was virtually careening down a black diamond slope—something she'd never done in real life. Her heart pounded as the computerized terrain flew past, taking her off big jumps and down sheer inclines. She popped into a virtual ollie and soared off a huge berm, then wiped out.

"That was great!" Bristol cried when Sanjay called for a break. She pulled off her VR goggles and rubbed her eyes. "But there weren't any obstacles."

39

"I thought you could use a straight shot," Sanjay said. "You look a little tired today."

"I'm fine," Bristol said quickly.

"How's the vision been?" Sanjay asked. "I noticed you haven't logged too many home exercises this week."

Bristol flushed. She'd activated the app but had only logged one short session for the week.

"I did more," she fibbed. "I just forgot to log them."

"No problem," Sanjay said. "It's a learning curve."

Bristol felt terrible that he'd accepted the lie so easily. But she pushed aside the guilt and followed Sanjay over to work on the letter ball exercise.

Everything she had to do whirled in her mind. Study. Homework. Coaching. Snowboarding. Vision therapy.

She was managing . . . right?

CHAPTER 5

AN IMPOSSIBLE CHOICE

Bristol woke up at six-thirty on Saturday morning. She'd stayed up late the night before doing a double home exercise session, not stopping until she had a headache.

She stretched and yawned, enjoying the cheerful glow of the colorful fairy lights in her room. Like usual, her eyes saw each strand as two. They were large and fuzzy-looking until she put on her glasses and gave her eyes time to focus.

Bristol hopped out of bed. The sun wouldn't rise until nearly eleven o'clock this time of year, but she'd be long gone by then. The ski shuttle picked up at nine o'clock at the end of her street.

I can't wait to spend the entire day on the slopes!

When Bristol came down with her gear bag, her parents were at the table, grading papers.

"You're up early," she remarked, grabbing bread to make toast. Her parents often slept in on Saturdays. Plus, they'd driven to Anchorage last night for a university lecture.

Her dad set down his coffee. "We need to talk, Bee."

Uh-oh.

"That sounds scary," Bristol joked. "Did Isla change majors again?"

Bristol's older sister was at college in Oregon. She could never decide whether to major in linguistics, Elizabethan studies, or classics. They all sounded equally boring to Bristol.

Mom frowned. "You can put that away," she said, looking at the Bristol's gear bag. "You're not snowboarding today."

"What?" Bristol cried. "I always board on Saturdays—that's part of our deal!"

"That deal also includes getting good grades." Her mom held up a paper.

Bristol groaned. Her English test!

"You snooped in my bag?" she demanded.

"I was looking for my travel mug," her dad interjected, "which was full of *someone's* old smoothie."

Bristol cringed. "It was just one test." Only now it was two bad grades.

She almost added that her eyes had been acting up even more than usual, especially with all the extra reading this semester. But that wouldn't convince her parents she could handle everything. If anything, it would just make them worry more.

Mom sighed. "We know you have some tough classes this year. But you have to prioritize. Maybe start spending more weekends studying."

"The mountain will wait, Bee," Dad added.

"The games are in three weeks!" Bristol protested. "I need to practice!"

"But isn't it just an exhibition run?" her dad asked. "Not exactly high stakes, right?"

Bristol scowled. They didn't understand. They'd never had to fight to get back to doing something they loved—and nearly lost.

"What about my students?" she demanded. "Class is at eleven. Greta's counting on me!"

Her parents exchanged a look, and Bristol's heart fluttered hopefully. They could hardly argue with honoring a commitment—that was part of responsibility, right?

"Fine," Mom finally said. "You can coach this morning. Then come straight home and study. I'll pick you up."

Bristol started to protest, but she knew that look in her mom's eyes. "Fine," she muttered, grabbing her toast and hurrying out the door.

* * *

On the slopes, Bristol and Jyoti got to help Aurora
use the DuoRider. The design of the frame gave
enough support—but not too much.

After several practice runs, Aurora squealed when
she made it down the hill solo. "I did it!" she cried.

Jyoti grinned. "You'll crush that exhibition run
at the games," she said. "Have you registered yet,
Bristol?"

Bristol adjusted her goggles. "I will." She felt a
rush of frustration, remembering the conversation
with her parents that morning.

Why can't they understand what this means to me?
Bristol thought angrily.

She wished she could talk to Isla about it, but her
big sister was an academic, just like their parents. Isla
never had to worry about disappointing them.

"Want to head to Minerva after lunch?" Jyoti
asked.

Bristol sighed. "Can't. Mom's picking me up."

As the kids made their way down the bunny slope, Bristol made a few wide, sweeping carves while facing uphill. She squinted wistfully at the higher peaks above.

Why did it seem like she had to choose? There had to be a way to balance school, coaching, and her own snowboarding goals, right?

There must be, Bristol told herself. *I just haven't found it yet.*

* * *

Bristol's mom was waiting in the lodge when class finished. Greta rushed over.

"Great to see you, Dr. Budnikas," she said. "I've been wanting to tell you what a great job Bristol's been doing with the kids. She's a natural!"

Bristol's mom looked surprised. "That's great," she said. "We've been worried she's overcommitting."

Bristol groaned. *Mom!*

But Greta nodded. "I remember when I first started coaching. I loved it so much I practically forgot everything else. My parents worried about my time management too."

"Did they?" Bristol's mom asked.

"Oh, yeah. It was hard for them to understand what it meant to me at first," Greta said. "But they finally got it." She nodded at Bristol. "I can't wait for you to see Bristol at the PowderX Games. You'll see what an amazing kids' coach she is."

Bristol smiled at Greta gratefully.

"And we're all excited about the exhibition runs," Greta continued. "We won't raise the profile of adaptive boarding overnight, but the more of us out there on the slopes, the more we can push for more competition categories."

"That's right, Mom," Bristol chimed in.

Bristol's mom sighed, but she was smiling. "Okay, you two. Good sales pitch." She turned to Bristol.

"You can do the games. *If* you do well on the next test. Otherwise, you might have a choice to make—coaching and your own boarding."

"There's another test in two weeks," Bristol assured her. "I'll be ready for it."

"Bring home a B plus," Mom said. "That's the deal."

"You got it," Bristol said confidently. "Seriously. Thanks, Mom. This really means a lot. I won't let you down."

* * *

As soon as they got home, Bristol went up to her room and studied all afternoon. She worked so hard that she didn't take the rest breaks Sanjay recommended for long study sessions.

When she finished, she was caught up, but her eyes were exhausted. She did a few of the vision therapy exercises on her app—tracking, convergence, divergence.

They all went terribly. Her eyes could barely focus and the double vision was intense. Bristol even felt a little nauseated from the exercises, which hadn't happened for a long time.

Great, she thought miserably. *This is the opposite of progress!*

"Ready for bed?" Mom asked, appearing in Bristol's doorway. "You've worked hard today. I'm proud of you. But it's almost ten."

"Just wrapping up," Bristol said, rubbing her eyes. She wondered if she should tell her mom about her eyes.

No, she decided. *I need to show her I can handle everything.*

CHAPTER 6

LOSING CONTROL

I've got this.

Bristol adjusted her goggles, double-checked her bindings, and took a deep breath. The curving, mogul-strewn surface of Minerva stretched out like a patchwork quilt. The overhead slope lights cast shadows on the snowy hill.

It was late afternoon on Friday, and Bristol had studied nonstop all week. She *had* to do well on her English test next week. She'd stayed up until midnight and set her alarm for six in the morning.

She was managing—but she was exhausted.

But today, she'd come to the mountain straight from her after-school study group. Her parents had allowed it since she'd been studying so hard.

Her mom's voice echoed in Bristol's mind as she prepared herself for the run. *You can do the games. If you do well on the next test. . . . That's the deal.*

I'll show them, Bristol told herself. *Once Mom and Dad see me do well in the games, they'll understand how much all this means to me!*

Bristol pointed her board downhill, breathed deep, and pushed off. Like always, that first rush of speed made her heart pound.

She scanned the slope for obstacles and other skiers and boarders, but the mountain was almost empty. Most people headed home or to the lodge when the daylight started to fade.

Still, Bristol was cautious. Her eyes were extra tired from lack of sleep and almost-constant reading. The darkened slope, while nearly empty, was spotted with shadows that made it tough to pick out the moguls.

The bright overhead lights didn't help, either. Bristol saw each light as two bright splotches. Even her specialized goggles, which usually helped reduce the double vision, weren't doing the trick.

It's okay, Bristol told herself. *I'll take it easy.*

She'd tackled Minerva plenty of times. And her focus was usually decent close-up. She'd keep her eyes on the terrain right in front of her.

Bristol stuck to the side of the run that wasn't as steep. After a full day of use, the snow was packed and slick in places.

As she entered the first stretch of moguls, her body tensed, ready to respond. These moguls were easy, small and gently curved on top.

Bristol focused on a spot just a few feet ahead. She shifted and hopped, coaxing her board from top to top like a bug skipping over water.

As she cleared the first mogul field, Bristol felt a rush of triumph. She knew these slopes, this hill. She belonged out here.

The next section was smooth but required skill. There were tighter curves and small, sheer drops to navigate.

Bristol glanced down the slope, squinting against the doubled images of the trail lights. She carved up and around a curve and continued to the first drop-off. Then she crouched low, shifted her weight, and popped her board's nose up for a perfect landing.

Yes! Bristol cheered silently. She kept cruising, picking up speed as she aimed for the next drop.

But then Bristol glanced into the distance to gauge how far she had to go. Immediately, the single images turned into two, throwing off her depth perception.

Stay cool.

But the slopes were almost completely dark now, and Bristol's overtired eyes simply wouldn't focus. What if she missed the drop-off because she was looking at the wrong image?

In a sudden panic, Bristol dug in and stopped, showering icy snow. This had been a bad idea.

Maybe I shouldn't have come up alone, she thought, annoyed with herself. After all, long-distance focusing was always challenging for her, especially in the dark. And that was when she *wasn't* exhausted from studying and lack of sleep.

But this was her first chance to practice all week. She'd spent so many hours staring at books and her computer that her eyes felt worse than ever out on the slopes.

It's not fair, Bristol thought angrily. Why did it feel like she had to choose one or the other? Close-up focus for school or long-distance focus for the slopes?

"Bristol!" someone called.

Bristol glanced up as Greta pulled up beside her.

"Working on the moguls?" the coach asked.

"Yeah," Bristol said. "Trying to, anyway."

Greta nodded. "Me too. I think one of my feet needs an adjustment," she said cheerfully. "I see my prosthetist Monday, thank goodness!"

Bristol didn't respond. Greta looked concerned.

"Everything okay?" she asked. "Don't you usually come up with Lita and Jyoti when it's dark?"

Bristol sighed. "Yeah." She pulled off her goggles and rubbed her eyes. "They had plans today, and I just wanted to get in some practice. The day never seems long enough."

Greta gave her a long look, then smiled. "Want to finish the run together?" she suggested. "Probably safer for us both, right?"

"Okay." Bristol suspected Greta could navigate the moguls just fine—prosthetic troubles or not. But she was glad the other coach had shown up.

They made their way through the next mogul field, going slowly and carefully. Bristol stayed behind Greta, using the other coach's bright-blue parka as a reference point. She kept close enough that her eyes could focus on it, but it was still hard.

"Darn!" Bristol yelled, almost missing a mogul in the shadows. She scrambled to shift her weight, nearly wiping out.

Greta stopped to let Bristol catch up. "Lose your balance?"

"I'm good," Bristol assured her. "But I think I'll skip the rest of the moguls."

Bristol finished the run cautiously, keeping to the edge and avoiding the remaining moguls. Greta's question echoed in her mind.

All I ever do is work on balance, Bristol thought.

Ever since her accident, she'd worked so hard. She'd gone through surgeries, scrambled to make up the school she'd missed, and done tons of physical and vision therapy. She'd pushed herself to regain as much sight and balance as possible.

She'd gotten back into sports, even though the sport she'd fallen in love with didn't even have an adaptive competition category for her disability. She'd stuck with it, even when she'd had to come to terms with the fact that she might never fully recover everything she'd lost.

Bristol had never stopped trying to balance it all.

Balancing her body, balancing her commitments, balancing what she wanted with what her parents expected.

But right now, nothing felt very balanced.

CHAPTER 7

A TINY LIE

Bristol doubled down, reading and studying as hard as she could. Her English test was Friday. The PowderX Games—and the exhibition runs—were the week after that.

She had to be ready. She needed a good grade. Everything depended on it!

In the kids' class on Tuesday afternoon, Bristol's students couldn't stop talking about the upcoming games.

"Will you and Jyoti race each other?" Jamila asked. "I bet you'll win, Bristol!"

"Will not!" Aurora piped up. "Jyoti will!"

Bristol and Jyoti chuckled. Each little girl was clearly dedicated to her favorite junior coach.

"Lucky for us," Jyoti said, "Bristol and I won't be in the same category. I'll be in the SB9 group—athletes with disabilities in one upper and one lower limb."

"That's right," Bristol added. "And I'm doing an exhibition run, just like you guys!"

Both Jamila and Aurora looked relieved. "That's good," Jamila declared. "We can root for you both!"

Bristol laughed. "Always," she joked, tugging the pom-pom on Jamila's hat. "As long I'm still your favorite! I'm just glad I won't have to race against you in a few years. You're going to rule the slopes!"

The coaches helped the kids practice weaving around obstacle flags. Aurora was getting the hang of the DuoRider, and her confidence was soaring.

This really is important, Bristol thought proudly. She looked around the slope and the gaggle of giggling kids. *And I deserve to keep being part of it.*

* * *

On Wednesday afternoon, Bristol studied on the way to vision therapy. Reading in the car made her queasy, but she needed all the study time she could get.

"I'm proud of you," her mom said as they drove the snowy roads toward Anchorage. "You've done a great job prioritizing these past couple weeks."

Bristol felt a rush of relief at her mom's words. *They haven't noticed I've been having more trouble with my eyes.*

"Piece of cake," she said lightly.

"That new vision therapy app seems neat," her mom added, glancing at Bristol's phone. "Must make it easy to record your exercises."

Bristol gazed out the window at the mountains. She had been logging exercises in the app every day. But she hadn't actually been *doing* them. She knew it was wrong. But her eyes were already so tired from all the extra reading and studying. Surely it would be okay for a little bit?

Bristol felt a guilty stab but nodded anyway. "It sure does."

I just need to get through the games, she told herself silently. *Then I'll get right back on track.*

But halfway through her appointment, Sanjay paused. "Have the home exercises been going okay?"

Bristol nodded. "Um . . . yeah. Why?"

Sanjay glanced down at his computer screen, where he could view the information in Bristol's app. "You've logged plenty of practice time, but you seem to be struggling a little more here in the clinic than what you've written down for at home."

Bristol shifted uncomfortably. "Oh, weird," she said. It wasn't *exactly* a lie, right?

Sanjay frowned. "It's just that you seem to have lost ground with a few of the ones we've done today," he said, glancing back at the app. "But it says here you've done them without any trouble."

He studied Bristol. "You know it's okay to dial things back if it's too much, right? Vision rehab isn't always a straight line of progress. There are ups and downs, especially after a head injury."

Bristol nodded, feeling rotten. She'd seen Sanjay for VT for more than three years now. He'd always made it clear that sometimes you couldn't force the exercises, which was frustrating. It seemed unfair that hard work didn't always guarantee results.

"I've just had a lot of homework," she said, trying to change the subject. "I have to do well on my English test or my parents won't let me do the games. They might even make me stop coaching altogether."

Sanjay nodded. "That's a lot," he said sympathetically. He handed Bristol a pair of red-green anti-suppression glasses. They were used for exercises to help both eyes work together. "How has your vision been on the slopes? Any new trouble?"

Bristol hesitated, almost ready to tell Sanjay the truth. How all the reading and studying this semester were straining her eyes. How her long-distance focus was worse than usual.

But what if Mom asks Sanjay how I'm doing in VT? Bristol worried. She couldn't risk that—not right before the games.

"No," she said finally, looking away to put on the practice glasses. "I'm fine."

The lie tasted bitter in her mouth.

CHAPTER 8

COMING CLEAN

On Friday, Bristol woke up with her stomach churning. Her test was today!

I'm ready, she told herself fiercely. She rubbed her tired eyes and dragged herself out of bed. *I have to be.*

The school day seemed to drag on forever. Finally, it was time for fifth period.

Ms. Lopez-Sørensen handed out the exams. "This is a big part of your grade," she reminded the class. "Take your time."

Bristol swallowed hard. She flipped the paper over, took a deep breath, and began.

The true-false section and multiple choice questions were first. Bristol checked and double-checked to make sure she'd filled in the circles correctly.

Next up was the written section. That was harder. Bristol was so tired it was tough to string her thoughts together. She worked feverishly, putting her pen down exactly as the bell rang.

Bristol knew she should feel relieved. But all she felt was overwhelmed with worry. If her grade wasn't good enough to satisfy her parents, everything would be ruined.

* * *

Bristol was on edge all weekend, fearing the worst about her test. She tried to distract herself. Staying caught up with her other classes. Coaching the Saturday kids' class. Taking a few practice runs of her own down the mountain.

By Sunday afternoon, she was feeling desperate. She dove into cleaning her room with a vengeance.

"Whoa," her dad said, coming upstairs. "Who are you, and what have you done with my daughter?"

Bristol flopped onto her bed. She hesitated, then blurted out the truth.

"I'm worried about my test," she admitted. She immediately froze, wishing she could take back the words.

Dad looked thoughtful. "Come on," he said, nodding down the hall. "Time for some therapeutic refreshment."

Bristol followed her dad to the kitchen. He made two mugs of peppermint cocoa. Then he gave her a searching look.

"Something's on your mind, Bee," he said. "I can always tell."

Bristol sipped her cocoa and sighed. "It's just everything, Dad." Part of her wanted to keep hiding her worries, but it was getting harder and harder.

"Your eyes have been bothering you, huh."

It wasn't a question.

Bristol was shocked. "How'd you know?"

Dad took another sip. "I wasn't born yesterday, kiddo," he said. "You're rubbing your eyes constantly, squinting all the time. Plus I've seen your bedroom light on past midnight all week."

Bristol sighed. "Does Mom know?"

Dad nodded. "She mentioned it to me last night."

Bristol gripped her mug. "You both said I can't snowboard—or coach—if I don't get everything right. And I'm trying *so* hard."

Her dad frowned. "We said you had to get *everything* right?"

Bristol thought back. "Mom sort of implied it," she finally said. "And neither of you care anything about sports."

Dad laughed. "True enough," he agreed. "I have no idea where you got your amazing athletic abilities."

Bristol couldn't help giggling. Her parents could just about make it down the bunny slope. But then she turned serious.

"Sometimes I wish I loved the same things you do," she admitted. "It would make things a lot easier. But I've always just *belonged* in sports. That's part of what was so awful about getting hurt. This thing I was great at was just . . . gone. I had to work so hard to get back to snowboarding. And school got even harder."

"I know, Bee," Dad said. "We know how hard you work."

"Then you should know why this exhibition run is important," Bristol said. "It might not sound like much, but one day I want to be able to compete in adaptive snowboarding. *Really* compete. And this is a tiny way I can help work toward that."

As she said it, Bristol realized that coaching the kids felt that way too. Like something positive she could do *now*.

"We're so proud of you, Bristol," her dad said seriously. "And clearly we need to do a better job of showing you that. Let's see how your test comes back, okay? Then we'll go from there."

"Okay," Bristol said, feeling a tiny bit better. It wasn't everything, but it was a start.

* * *

When Bristol walked into English class on Monday, a stack of graded tests sat on Ms. Lopez-Sørensen's desk. Bristol's heart started pounding. She could barely concentrate during class.

Finally, just before the bell rang, the teacher handed back the tests. Bristol stared at hers for a long moment before cautiously turning it over.

Relief surged through her when she saw the red B+ on top. Just high enough to keep her on the slopes! Then she yawned, a reminder of too many late nights.

Even if I'm tired, Bristol thought, *I'm balancing it all!*

* * *

At dinner that night, Bristol showed her parents her grade. "I know it's not an A," she said quickly, knowing their high standards.

Mom finished her salad and set down her fork. "Ms. Lopez-Sørensen called today," she said, looking serious.

Bristol's heart dropped. "You said I could keep boarding if I got a B plus!" she protested. "That was the deal, right?"

"She didn't call about your grade," Mom said. "She was worried. She said you've seemed really stressed at school and wanted to know if there was anything going on. Is there?"

Bristol opened her mouth to say everything was fine. Then she caught her dad's eye.

"You can talk to us," he said. "Just tell the truth."

Bristol took a deep breath. "I've been really tired from staying up late to study," she finally admitted.

71

"But I had to! I don't know what I'll do if I have to give up boarding and coaching. It means *everything* to me!"

Bristol's parents exchanged a long look.

"Dad told me about your talk," Mom said slowly. "It's true, we might not understand it, exactly. But we've seen such a huge leap in your maturity this year, especially since you started coaching. Ms. Lopez-Sørensen mentioned how much her nephew loves your classes."

"We want to help you work out a balance, Bee," Dad added. "But you have to let us know if you're struggling, okay?"

Bristol took a deep breath. "I have been," she admitted. "My vision's been all over the place lately. I even fibbed to Sanjay about doing my home exercises." She looked down, embarrassed.

Her mom nodded. "Your teacher mentioned your vision too," she said. "She suggested maybe getting back on a five-oh-four plan and getting your textbooks in audio format. Then you wouldn't need to strain your eyes so much."

"But wouldn't that be taking the easy way out?" Bristol asked uncertainly.

She'd had a 504 plan that gave her extra accommodations at school after her accident. But hadn't needed any for about a year now.

Her parents both shook their heads. "Bee," her dad said kindly, "we've *never* known you to take the easy way out."

Bristol smiled. Then she remembered what Greta had said when they were demoing the new equipment. *Adaptations are just a way to get what you need to do what you love.*

Bristol realized she never questioned it when her students needed adaptive equipment or extra help. Maybe she owed herself the same. Maybe she should trust her parents a little more too—even with the hard stuff.

CHAPTER 9

FINDING BALANCE

Bristol felt a prick of disappointment as she pushed off at the top of the chairlift. Taking a deep breath, she pushed her board past the turnoff to Minerva's mogul fields.

Soon, she told herself firmly. *Just not today.*

Bristol firmly turned her board toward the top of Vesta. The gentle slope had been transformed into a banked slalom run, full of wide, horizontal curves. Tomorrow, snowboarders would be flying down it for both competition and exhibition runs.

Bristol wouldn't be with them.

After talking to her parents and Greta—and confessing to Sanjay about lying on the vision therapy app—Bristol had made a hard decision about her own participation in the games.

As much as she wanted to tackle an exhibition run tomorrow, she'd realized that now wasn't the right time. Her eyes didn't feel strong enough to do a fast run on a slope packed with spectators, camera flashes, and other visual distractions.

She'd be okay on the bunny slope with the kids. But she wouldn't be able to do her best up here—not by tomorrow.

After thinking it over, Bristol had decided to hold off. Not forever. Just until she got back on track with vision therapy and school and everything else.

But she was here now. The trails were technically closed to be groomed and readied for the games. But Greta had convinced the groomers to let Bristol take a solo run. No obstacles. No people. Just her and the silent, snowy slope.

Bristol adjusted her goggles and glanced down the run. As usual, the farther ahead she looked, the more everything went double.

But for now, Bristol decided, she was done stressing out about things too far down the path for her to control. Whether her vision would ever fully recover. Whether there'd ever be a competition classification that would match her abilities. Whether she'd meet the expectations and hopes of everyone else in her life.

For now, she was going to focus on the things that were right in front of her. Her students. Her family. Her snowboard. And finding the perfect balance between them all—her way.

Bristol carved down the slope in strong, powerful curves, popping an ollie off a side bank. The rushing wind stung her cheeks. The *shhhh-shhhing* of her snowboard edge sliced through the snow.

She crouched low and banked into the first turn, nearly brushing the orange safety fencing but well under control. She kept her focus close, relaxing her eyes and scanning the powder just ahead of her.

The next traverse was a little steeper, a little faster. Bristol settled into her rhythm. Her board felt like an extension of her body, strong and balanced and sure.

Bristol leaned into the next bank. She cut it a little close on the turn but recovered her balance and flew down the last curves, ending with a perfect rush at the base of the slope.

Greta was waiting at the bottom. "You crushed it!" she said, offering a high five.

"Thanks," Bristol said, slapping Greta's glove. "I really needed that."

Bristol unbuckled one binding and towed her board as she and Greta headed off the slopes toward the parking lot. They were going to get lunch together before Greta dropped her off at home.

"And thanks for understanding about the exhibition," Bristol added.

She'd been afraid to let Greta down by not doing the exhibition run. She should have known better.

"Absolutely," Greta said. "I'm sorry if I made you feel pressured. I never meant to do that."

"I know. And I really do want to be able to compete one day . . ." Bristol started.

Greta smiled. "But you also have a life to live in the meantime."

Bristol smiled back. "Exactly. And I'm still super excited about the kids' run tomorrow. I should be able to manage the bunny slope, even with all the crowds."

"How are your eyes doing?" Greta asked. She opened the trunk of her car so Bristol could load her snowboard.

"Still being a pain," Bristol replied. "But I talked about it with my vision therapist—and my teachers—and we're making a new plan. Might need to make some adjustments for a while. But I can still coach."

"I'm so glad," Greta said. "I know I've said it before, but you really are a natural with the kids.

And all the adaptive gear we use with them. Who knows where that could take you?"

"Down the bunny slope, I imagine," Bristol joked.

"Hopefully." Greta grinned. "Or maybe to a career in sports rehab or adaptive technology one day."

Bristol considered that as they climbed into the car. It was an interesting thought.

"Maybe," she said. "Right now, the only place I want to be led is wherever you're taking us for lunch. Coach buys, right?"

CHAPTER 10

LET THE GAMES BEGIN!

"All right, team!" Greta yelled cheerfully at the bottom of the chairlift. "This is it! Who's ready to shred that bunny slope?"

"Me! Me!" the kids hollered.

The PowderX Games were finally here, and it was almost time for the kids' class to make their exhibition run. They were off-the-charts excited.

Jamila bounced excitedly as they waited for the chairlift. "I can't wait! I can't wait!" she squealed.

Bristol couldn't blame her. The atmosphere of the competition was infectious. Everyone was so positive and supportive. A big crowd had turned out for the games. People in winter gear milled around, spectating or buying or getting ready for their own races.

Bristol knew her parents were somewhere in the crowd too. The thought made her stomach flutter. Even though she wasn't competing today, she was equal parts nervous and excited.

A moment later, the chairlift arrived. It scooped up Bristol and Jamila and towed them to the top of the mountain.

Bristol glanced down at the setup below. Overnight, Roman's Run had been transformed.

Portable tents and sound systems dotted the bottoms of different slopes, which were studded with racing flags and portable starting gates. Gear companies and other sponsors had tables with stuff for sale. There was even a display of the latest innovations in adaptive equipment.

I need to check that out later, Bristol thought.

"Remember what Greta said this morning," Bristol said as the lift climbed higher. "There's going to be lots of commotion today. You might have to work harder to stay focused on the slopes."

"Nah." Jamila grinned. "I was made for the spotlight!"

Bristol grinned. "You can say that again!"

At the top of the lift, Bristol spotted Jamila as they got off. Then she helped Greta and Jyoti gather the rest of the kids together at the top of the bunny slope. When they were ready, Greta gave the announcer a thumbs-up.

"And now," the voice boomed over the loudspeaker, "let's give it up for Roman Run's very own Tiny Titans—the skiers and snowboarders of the next generation!"

Seeing the excitement on each of her students' faces as their names were called out made Bristol's heart swell with pride. They'd all gained so much confidence over the past weeks.

Bristol made sure Jamila had her outriggers. Jyoti double-checked Aurora's alignment in the DuoRider. Greta and the rest of the senior coaches made sure that everyone else was ready. Then, with the cameras rolling and the crowd cheering, they all headed down the slope together.

The shouts of encouragement from the spectators made the kids even more excited. Jamila grinned from ear-to-ear as she carved down the hill. Bristol only had to scramble once to collect the outrigger the little girl dropped to wave at her parents.

Aurora, who had gotten more and more comfortable with the DuoRider, glided down the mountain. She flushed with excitement when one of the older racers high-fived her at the bottom of the run.

Pretty perfect, Bristol thought proudly.

At the base of the hill, the kids and coaches hugged each other. The kids' parents clustered around to take pictures.

"Way to go!" Greta exclaimed. "I'm so proud of you all!"

"So are we."

Bristol swung around. Her parents were there, smiling at her.

"I can see why you love this, Bee," Mom continued. "And how good you are at it too."

"How're your eyes feeling?" Dad asked.

"They're okay," Bristol assured him.

It was true. Her eyes were feeling better since she'd started using the audio textbooks for some of her classes. Sanjay had adjusted her vision therapy program too. She had work to do, but now she felt more in control of things.

Greta glided over. "What'd you think?" she asked Bristol's parents. "Did they wow you?"

"They sure did." Bristol's mom smiled over at the kids, but her eyes were on Bristol. "You looked so confident out there, Bee," she added. "Your dad and I both saw it. You're a teacher at heart. Just like us!"

Bristol blinked. She'd never thought of it that way. All this time, she'd been so sure that her parents could never understand or appreciate what she did on the slopes. But maybe they really weren't so different, after all.

Bristol's eyes suddenly felt a little watery and not from the chilly wind off the mountain. "Thanks, Mom," she said. "Does that mean we'll get you on a board next season?" she added jokingly.

Her parents both laughed. "Possibly," her mom said. "But only if you bring home B-pluses or better next semester!"

"Deal," Bristol declared, laughing. "It'll be worth the extra studying to see that!"

GLOSSARY

academic (ak-uh-DEM-ik)—a form of schooling in which students learn information rather than hands-on skills

adaptive (uh-DAP-tiv)—designed or intended to assist people of all abilities

ancient (AYN-shunt)—from a long time ago

atmosphere (AT-muhss-feer)—a surrounding influence or set of conditions

berm (BURM)—a banked turn or corner on a downhill ski slope

cerebral palsy (suh-REE-bruhl PAWL-zee)—a condition resulting from damage to the brain before, during, or shortly after birth that can affect muscle coordination, balance, speech, or other body functions

chairlift (CHAIR-lift)—a line of chairs attached to a moving cable that carries people to the top of a mountain

depth perception (DEPTH pur-SEP-shuhn)—the ability to sense how far away something is or how much space is between things

exhibition (ek-suh-BIH-shuhn)—a public display where athletes show off their skills

fatigue (fuh-TEEG)—great tiredness

incline (IN-kline)—a slope

infectious (in-FEK-shuhss)—easily spread to others

mogul (MOH-guhl)—a bump in a ski run

ollie (AH-lee)—a trick in which a snowboarder shifts weight to the tail of the board to make the board spring into the air

prosthetic (pross-THET-ik)—a manufactured part that takes the place of a lost or absent body part, such as an arm or leg

slalom (SLAH-luhm)—an individual alpine race around obstacles

terrain (tuh-RAYN)—the surface of the land

traverse (truh-VURS)—a crossing

tripod (TRYE-pod)—a trick that involves a snowboarder riding down the slope with both hands and front of the board in the snow and the tail of the board in the air

DISCUSSION QUESTIONS

1. Bristol doesn't feel like her athletic interests match those of her family. Where do we see this lead to conflict or misunderstanding? Are there any instances where it could have been avoided?

2. Throughout this story, Bristol struggles with balancing her many commitments and interests. Talk about what "balance" might mean in different people's lives. What does it mean for you?

3. Bristol is passionate about teaching other kids with disabilities how to snowboard. Why is this so important to her? Look back through the story for specific instances to support your answer.

WRITING PROMPTS

1. Twice in this story Bristol takes a solo run down the slopes. Write a paragraph about how you think she's feeling the first time, then one about how you think she's feeling the second time.

2. As Bristol tries to manage her struggles with school and vision therapy, she hides things from several people in her life, including Sanjay and her parents. How could she have handled those situations differently? Choose one such incident and rewrite it so that Bristol tells the truth from the start.

3. Even though Bristol snowboards with a visual impairment, there isn't an adaptive snowboarding classification in which she can compete. Write about a time when you felt that there wasn't a place or way for you to participate in something you wanted to be part of.

Snowboarding first got its start in the United States back in 1917, when a creative kid named Vern Wicklund stood up on a sled and zoomed down a snowy Minnesota hill. In the 1960s, a dad in Michigan invented the "Snurfer" by attaching two skis to a single steering mechanism. In mountainous regions of Austria and Turkey, there are stories of people riding sideways on boards to travel through deep snow as far back as 400 years ago.

Adaptive snowboarding—or para snowboarding— was first included at the 2014 Paralympic Games in Sochi, Russia, and continues to grow in popularity. Unfortunately, there are currently only three classifications allowed to compete at the Paralympic level:

SBLL1: lower limb impairment (more severe)

SBLL2: lower limb impairment (less severe)

BBUL: upper limb impairment

This means that only some adaptive snowboarders have the chance to aim toward the highest levels of competition. Others—like boarders with impaired vision or balance—do not.

However, the International Paralympic Committee (IPC) has recognized that the sport is still evolving. There is hope that more classifications will be added in the future, expanding competition access to more disabled snowboarders.

Almost any sport can be modified to allow people of all abilities to participate—snowboarding is no exception. The American Association of Snowboard Instructors (AASI) offers special programs to train and certify instructors. This allows them to use adaptive techniques and equipment to teach snowboarding to people of varying physical or cognitive abilities.

To learn more about adaptive snowboarding, check out these websites:

International Paralympic Committee
paralympic.org

National Paralympic Heritage Trust
paralympicheritage.org.uk/snowboarding

Professional Ski Instructors of America/American Association of Snowboard Instructors (PSIA AASI)
thesnowpros.org

Smithsonian: A Brief History of Snowboarding
smithsonianmag.com/innovation/brief-history-snowboarding-180979233

World Snowboard Federation
worldsnowboardfederation.org

LOOKING FOR MORE
SNOWBOARDING ACTION?
THEN PICK UP ...

JAKE MADDOX JV

SNOWBOARD
SHAM